WHAT CAN I DO?

A Book for Children of Divorce

Published by
M A G I N A T I O N   P R E S S
An Educational Publishing Foundation Book
American Psychological Association
750 First Street, NE
Washington, DC 20002

For more information about our books, including a complete catalog,
please write to us, call 1-800-374-2721, or visit our website at
www.maginationpress.com.

Printed by Phoenix Color Corporation, Hagerstown, MD

Library of Congress Cataloging-in-Publication Data

Lowry, Danielle.
What Can I Do? : a book for children of divorce / by Danielle Lowry ;
illustrated by Bonnie Matthews.
p.   cm.
Summary: A young girl tries everything she can think of to keep
her parents from getting a divorce, but with the help of a school counselor
she comes to realize that the divorce is not her fault.
ISBN 1-55798-770-X (soft : alk. paper) — ISBN 1-55798-769-6 (hc. : alk. paper)
[1. Divorce — Fiction. 2. Parent and child — Fiction.]
I. Matthews, Bonnie J., 1963- ill. II. Title.

PZ7.L96727 Wh 2001
[Fic] — dc21   2001030224
Manufactured in the United States of America
10 9 8 7 6 5 4 3 2

WHAT CAN I DO?

A Book for Children of Divorce

by Danielle Lowry
illustrated by Bonnie Matthews

MAGINATION PRESS • WASHINGTON, DC

Introduction

The purpose of this book is threefold. First and most importantly, it was written to help children help themselves through the experience of their parents' divorce by giving them a sense of empowerment in what is a powerless situation for them. When read by a child alone, the book suggests sources of support, as well as several concrete ways of coping during a confusing and emotional time. By following the thoughts and actions of the main character, the child is also helped to recognize and understand some of the feelings he or she may be experiencing.

Second, the book may be used as a counseling tool. As a school counselor, I see that children typically blame themselves for their parents' divorce, they often feel they have to "parent" their parents, and they feel very confused. I wrote this story to aid professionals who work with these children. It can be an effective counseling tool in group work both as an ice breaker and to initiate discussion at various phases of the main character's growth in awareness. The book also focuses on problem solving and the discussion of options. The various solutions in the story can serve as a springboard for the exchange of ideas among children in similar situations and facing similar dilemmas.

Finally, the book is a resource for parents. Divorcing parents may read the story with their child and use the opportunity to open lines of communication. In addition, *What Can I Do?* can serve to educate parents themselves about some of the issues that their child may be struggling with and that they may not be aware of.

It is my hope that this book will help children increase their resiliency in facing the difficult life transition of divorce—and possibly other difficulties down the road. It is also my hope that it will aid parents and professionals in helping children of divorce feel safe and supported.

DANIELLE LOWRY, M.S.

Contents

To J.B. with love,
Dani

For Melanie Kendall,
Love Aunt Bonnie

Chapter 1
The News

One day, Rosie's mom and dad told her they had some sad news. They asked Rosie to sit down with them on the sofa, and they told her they had decided to get a divorce. Rosie knew what the word *divorce* meant. She knew that it meant her mom and dad wouldn't be living together anymore. Her friend Karen's parents had gotten a divorce and no longer lived in the same house. Now Karen spent time with each of them, but not with them together.

Rosie's mom and dad explained that after this weekend, Rosie's dad would live in an apartment, and Rosie and her mom would stay in their house. Rosie's dad promised to visit every Saturday and told Rosie she could spend time with him on other days, if she wanted to.

Rosie wasn't listening. Her world had just fallen apart. Rosie kept wondering why this was happening, why her parents had decided to get a divorce. She wanted them to take it back, she wanted everything to be fixed. She knew her parents argued a lot. She often heard them fighting at night, after she was in bed.

But why did they have to get a divorce? Sometimes Rosie and her friends had fights, too. They might stay mad at each other for a whole day, but then they would make up and play together again.

"Why can't you two just make up?" Rosie asked. Rosie's mom shook her head. Her dad said, "Rosie, we've tried to work

out our problems, but our relationship
isn't healthy, and we think it is best if we
don't live together anymore."

When Rosie was alone in her room,
she curled up on the bed with Clementine,
her cat, and thought. She thought about
all the things her mom and dad had said.
She wondered what she could do to keep

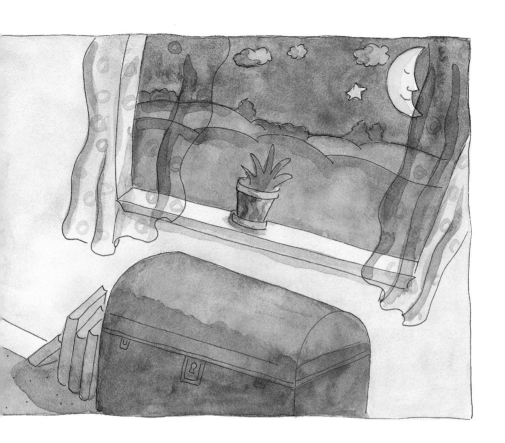

her parents from getting a divorce. She
didn't understand why their relationship
wasn't healthy or why they couldn't live
together anymore.

That night Rosie had trouble falling
asleep. "If they're not healthy," she
thought, "that means they're sick." The
next day, Rosie watched her mom and dad

very closely. They didn't look sick.
They still got dressed in the morning and
went to work. They didn't go to the doctor
and get medicine, either. "Maybe they're
not sick after all," Rosie thought.

Rosie did think that they looked sad,
though, and sometimes she found one of
them crying. Rosie thought there must be
something she could do to keep them
together. She thought and thought, and
soon she had a plan.

Chapter 2
The Plan

"I know what I'll do!" said Rosie, smiling to herself. "I am going to cheer Mom and Dad up so they won't be so sad. That will be easy. I'm really good at cheering people up." Rosie decided to be her silliest, funniest, and happiest self whenever she was around her mom or dad.

The next day, Rosie saw her dad crying in his bedroom while he packed some of his things. She ran back to her room, got her baton and her trumpet, and put on a grand, one-person marching band show just for him. "Look at me, Daddy," she sang. Her dad laughed and hugged her, but he still seemed sad.

One night after dinner, Rosie saw her mom sitting all alone at the kitchen table. Rosie thought her mom looked lonely and needed some silly company. She decided to tell her best knock-knock joke.

"Knock-knock!" said Rosie.

"Oh, honey, not now, okay?" her mom answered.

"Come on, Mom, say 'Who's there,'" Rosie urged.

"Rosie, please stop. I'm not in the mood right now for knock-knock jokes. Why don't you go and play?"

Rosie yelled back, "I was only trying to cheer you up. If you and Daddy are so sad about getting a divorce, maybe you shouldn't get one!"

Rosie's mom hugged her and said she

was sorry. "We are sad," she said, "but it is still best that we get a divorce. You must be sad, too, I know. This will be hard on all of us for a while."

Things weren't going exactly as Rosie had planned, but she wasn't ready to give up. She thought about the things

her parents fought about. She remembered that sometimes they fought about money. They argued about what to buy and who was spending too much. That gave Rosie an idea.

"I'll give them all the money in my piggy bank and all the birthday money

I get from Grandma and Grandpa, and I won't ask for an allowance anymore," she thought. "If I give them all my money, they won't have any more money problems. Then they won't fight so much, and they won't get a divorce!"

Rosie was pleased with her new idea. She emptied her piggy bank into a shoebox. She even used wrapping paper to decorate the box like a present. Then she left it on her parents' dresser.

The next morning, Rosie's mom and dad said, "Rosie, we really don't want you to give us your money. It is very kind and generous of you to offer it, but your money belongs to you."

Rosie felt a lump in her throat, and swallowed hard when they hugged her and gave her back her box. "I guess I will have to think of something else," she thought.

Chapter 3
Try Harder!

"Now what else can I do?" Rosie asked herself. She remembered that sometimes, when the house got really messy, her parents fought about whose job it was to keep the house clean. "I will clean my room and keep it extra neat so they won't get mad," Rosie thought. "I'll even clean the whole house after school! Then they'll be happy again, and dad won't move out."

Rosie cleaned and scrubbed and

polished. The house looked beautiful, and her room was perfect. Her mom and dad looked pleased. "Thank you for your hard work, Rosie," said her mom. "But you don't have to clean the whole house. That's a grown-up job. If you just do your usual chores like taking care of Clementine and helping with the dishes, that will be a great help."

"They are not *cooperating* with my plan!" thought Rosie, clenching her fists. "Now I just want to mess up the house all over again." She felt the lump come back in her throat, and ran away to look for Clementine.

On Saturday, when Rosie's dad moved out, the lump stayed there all day. Uncle Mike came to help him with his things. "I'll see you Monday night, and next weekend too," Rosie's dad promised her, giving her a kiss and hug. Then Rosie watched them drive away.

Rosie was sad, but she did not want

to give up trying to get her mom and dad back together. "I know what else I can do," Rosie thought. "I can try harder in school. Mom and Dad are always happy when I bring home a good report card. If they're happy, they definitely won't get a divorce, and maybe Dad will come home again."

Rosie's next report card wasn't as dazzling as she had hoped. It was good, mostly B's, but she had slipped from an A to a C in spelling. "I actually did worse, not better," thought Rosie. "That won't make things easier for Mom and Dad. They'll be more upset, and it's all my fault."

Rosie was very disappointed that her plan was not working. She also felt angry. "Let them get upset about my dumb report card," she thought, throwing her backpack on the floor. "I don't care. Why should I? They don't care about me or they wouldn't be getting a divorce!"

Chapter 4

Rosie Gives Up

For the next few weeks, Rosie felt so bad that she didn't act like herself. She didn't try as hard in school. She missed some homework assignments and failed a test in math. Rosie also decided she wasn't going to join the soccer team, something she had planned to do with her best friend, Bethany. Rosie told Bethany when she saw her in gym class.

"What do you mean you're not going to play soccer?" demanded Bethany.

"We've been practicing and practicing. We were going to be teammates!"

"I don't care," yelled Rosie. "I don't want to play soccer. It's a stupid game."

Bethany looked hurt and started to cry. Rosie called her a baby and ran out of the gym. By the time Rosie got back to her classroom, Mr. Harris had heard all about what happened from the gym

teacher. He told Rosie she should apologize to Bethany, which she did, and he said he wanted her to stay in during recess.

While she was sitting at her desk waiting for recess to end, Mr. Harris came to talk to her. "What's got you so upset, Rosie?" he asked softly. "It's not like you to yell at your friends and hurt their feelings. Is something wrong?"

Rosie started to cry. "Yes, Mr. Harris, something is wrong. My parents are getting a divorce," said Rosie. "I tried to be extra good so they would stay together, but it didn't work. My dad moved out anyway, and I really miss him."

Mr. Harris crouched down and looked into Rosie's sad little face. "Rosie, there is nothing you can do to get your mom and dad back together, because it's not your fault that they're getting a divorce. You can't fix this problem between your mom and your dad."

"It's not my fault." Rosie repeated the words to herself. She thought about this for a minute. Sometimes she did think it was her fault that her mom and dad were getting a divorce. If she had only behaved better, or kept her room cleaner, or gotten better grades, maybe they wouldn't have fought so much.

Mr. Harris suggested that tomorrow

Rosie meet with Ms. Gonzalez, the school counselor, to talk about her feelings. Rosie knew Ms. Gonzalez because she often talked to Rosie's class about how to get along with others and how to have good study skills. Rosie had never met with her alone, though. She was a little nervous about talking to her all by herself, but she agreed to see her the next day.

Chapter 5
Ms. Gonzalez

When Rosie walked into Ms.
Gonzalez's room, she forgot all about
being nervous. It was small and cozy.
A colorful puppet theater stood in the
corner, next to a shelf filled with toys and
books. A round table with chairs took up
the middle of the room.

"Hello, Rosie," Ms. Gonzalez greeted
her warmly. Thank you for coming to see
me." She invited Rosie to sit in a bright
blue beanbag chair next to the window.

"How are you feeling today?" she asked.

Rosie talked to Ms. Gonzalez for half an hour. It was much easier than she thought it would be. She told Ms. Gonzalez all about her parents' divorce and how hard she had worked to keep them together. Ms. Gonzalez listened,

then asked a few questions. When it was time for Rosie to go back to class, Ms. Gonzalez suggested that they meet again in a few days.

Rosie met with Ms. Gonzalez several times over the next few weeks. Sometimes she was sad and even cried. Sometimes

she was mad at her mom and dad.
Sometimes she was relieved that her
parents weren't together, because she
didn't wake up at night anymore and hear
them fighting or crying. And sometimes
she even felt guilty for feeling happy.
Rosie talked about how confused she was
having all of these feelings.

Rosie had lots of questions, too.
"What does it mean when a relationship
isn't healthy anymore?" Rosie asked Ms.
Gonzalez. "What should I tell my friends?
Will I always live with my mom? Is one of
my parents the big boss now and the other
one the little boss?"

Ms. Gonzalez listened to Rosie. "This
is a very confusing time for you, Rosie,"
she said. "I can understand why you have
lots of questions. Let's talk first about
what it means when a relationship isn't
healthy. Usually a relationship isn't healthy
anymore when people hurt each other's
feelings more than they make each

other happy. And that happens for a lot of different reasons. When people can't work out their differences, sometimes it's better that they live apart."

"You mean my mom and dad's relationship was unhealthy because they would fight and cry more than they would laugh together?" asked Rosie.

"Yes, Rosie, that can make for an unhealthy relationship—more sadness than happiness," answered Ms. Gonzalez.

"Who will take care of me?" asked Rosie. "Will I always live with my mom?"

"That's something you need to talk to your mom and dad about," answered Ms. Gonzalez. "They will decide whom you will live with and when you will visit the other parent. You might live with both parents the same amount of time, or you might spend more time with one parent than the other. Some families need a judge to help them figure this out. You can tell your mom and dad, or a judge, how you feel about the arrangements. This will help them decide what is best for you."

Chapter 6
All About Love

After talking with Ms. Gonzalez, Rosie started feeling a little better than she did before. But Rosie still had one more big worry. On the way to her after-school care one day, Rosie stared out the bus window and wondered, "If Mom and Dad's relationship could get sick, could their relationship with me get sick, too? I argue with them sometimes. What if they decide it's best to divorce me, too?"

Rosie was so sad and scared by the

time the bus dropped her off that she
didn't even want to play with her friends.
She pretended to do her homework, but
she couldn't concentrate.

When Rosie's mom arrived to pick her
up, Rosie ran to hug her. She looked as if
she was about to cry.

"Rosie, what's wrong? Did something

happen at school?" asked her mom.

Rosie got into the car and blurted out, "Can you or dad divorce me?"

"Neither one of us would ever want to divorce you," answered her mom. "Why would you ask that?"

Rosie answered, "Because I don't always do everything I'm supposed to do. I don't always clean my room, and sometimes I talk back. So maybe you and Dad won't want to live with me, either."

Rosie's mom pulled the car into a parking lot so she could look at Rosie. "First of all, Rosie, we both love you with all our hearts, and nothing can ever change that. Love between children and their moms and dads is different than love between mothers and fathers. The kind of love between children and their parents lasts forever, no matter what."

Rosie's mom continued. "We are able to take care of ourselves, Rosie. You are our child. It's our responsibility as parents

to take care of you and to help you grow
up healthy and safe whether we live
together or not. It's what we want to do.
Does this make any sense?"

Rosie nodded and said, "Kind of."

"Rosie, your dad and I disagree on
things that have nothing to do with you,
but we agree on this and always will. We

both love you and want to take care of you. That will never change. Ask your dad, too. I know he'll say the same thing."

The next Saturday, Rosie asked her dad the same question. Just like her mom did, he told her that they would always love her, no matter what. He also said she didn't have to behave perfectly or always get good grades to deserve this.

Rosie felt better, but she wondered how there could be different kinds of love. Then she thought about Clementine as they snuggled in bed together. "I love Clementine lots and lots and lots, she's like my best friend. But it is different from how I love my mom and dad. It's still love, just different." Rosie also thought, "I love Grandma and Grandpa, too, but that's still different from the way I love Mom and Dad." Rosie stroked Clementine's soft fur and whispered, "I guess maybe there are different kinds of love." Clementine purred.

Chapter 7

Questions and Answers

One day Ms. Gonzalez told Rosie that there were other children in school whose parents were divorced and that they met in her office once a week to talk about their feelings. She invited Rosie to join the group. Rosie asked her mom and dad if she could join, and they said yes.

The first time, Rosie did not know what to expect. After introducing Rosie,

Ms. Gonzalez suggested that they play the Wishing Well game. Rosie learned that this was one of the group's favorite games. Ms. Gonzalez gave each child three pennies and passed around a coffee can decorated like a stone well. The children made their wishes silently, then threw a penny into the well. They could make one, two, or three wishes. And if they wanted to, they could tell the group what they wished for.

"Would anyone like to share one of their wishes?" asked Ms. Gonzalez.

Sarah raised her hand. "I wish I knew

why my mom and dad wanted to get a divorce. I still don't really know the reason."

"Me too," said Jamel. "I don't get why my mom and dad split up."

"I wish my mom and dad could somehow get back together," said Whitney.

"I know what you mean," said Martin, "but my mom and dad fought all the time. The one good thing about the divorce is that I don't have to listen to that anymore. That's kind of a relief."

Rosie was amazed. "They sound just

like me," she thought. "They have the same questions and feelings that I do."

Rosie learned a lot from the children in the group. One day they all talked about where they lived. Rosie learned some new words. She learned that "custody" means who will care for them.

Whitney's parents had worked out a new custody arrangement for her. "My brother and I are going to live with my mom from Sunday night to Thursday, and then live with my dad from Thursday to Sunday night," said Whitney. "I know it sounds confusing, but it works best for us."

"I was doing something like that too, sort of half and half, until my mom moved back to California," said Jamel. "Now I live most of the time with my dad, and I go to visit my mom on holidays and vacations."

Rosie explained that she was going to live with her mom during the week and see her dad on the weekends. "I don't get to spend all the time I want to with my dad, but sometimes we get together during the week if I really miss him or if I have a soccer game or something. And sometimes I'll spend a weekend with my mom if we've been rushing around too much and need fun time together. So it works out okay," she told the group.

One day Rosie realized she had stopped asking, "What can I do to get my mom and dad back together?" Instead, she asked, "What can I do to help myself feel better?"

On the last day of school before summer vacation, Ms. Gonzalez asked Rosie what she had learned to do in case she started to feel sad again about her parents' divorce. Rosie thought for a minute and then said, "I can talk to my mom or dad or to a friend. It doesn't have to be a friend whose parents are divorced. It can be any friend who cares about me and who won't tell my private feelings to other kids."

"I can write a letter to my grandma and grandpa, or I can go out and play. I can read a story or draw a picture. I can even write a letter to myself about what I am feeling. I can take a walk with a friend or pet my cat, Clementine. When I'm staying with one of my parents and I miss the other one, I can draw a picture, or write a letter to give them, or call on the phone."

Sometimes Rosie still wished her

mom and dad would get back together, but she knew she couldn't make that happen. She also knew she might never understand why they got divorced. She just had to understand that it was grown-up stuff that she couldn't change. And most important, she knew that there were lots of things she could do to help herself feel better.

"Finally," thought Rosie, "I have some answers to the question *What can I do?*"

About the Author

DANIELLE LOWRY, M.S., earned her master's degree in Counselor Education from Syracuse University. As a school counselor for children in their early and middle years, and as a child of divorce herself, she knows intimately the feelings and questions that children confront when their parents separate.

"Kids do blame themselves, and they do want to fix things," she says, "even when they are told otherwise." In *What Can I Do?* the author takes the reader on a journey of trial and error in a search for answers that work. "I wrote this book to show young readers the resources that are available to them, and that they can access themselves. In my experience, this is particularly empowering for young children whose lives are very much decided and directed by adults."

Ms. Lowry lives in Upstate New York with her husband and daughter.

About the Illustrator

BONNIE MATTHEWS taught herself illustration while she was a student of graphic design at Virginia Commonwealth University. In addition to the many children's books she has illustrated, her whimsical people and animals have appeared in more than 100 magazines worldwide, and on gift wrap, greeting cards, tin cans, and even the cover of the *Land's End Kids* catalog.

Ms. Matthews donates part of her efforts to organizations she cares about, such as the Baltimore Zoo, the World Health Organization, the Wilderness Society, and Johns Hopkins Children's Center. She lives in Baltimore and is a frequent speaker at local elementary, middle, and high schools, where she encourages children to draw and follow their creative aspirations. "I have a special interest in children's books," she says, "because I think that pictures help promote reading, and I personally had a difficult time learning to read."